BUBBIES

Night of the Bubbies

Damien Casey

Cover by Joe Fogle
@cryptoteeology on Insta

Author's note that you really should read first because I, the author, would appreciate that greatly.

Before you ever dive into this thing, I want you to know this is a dumb book. This book is filled with dad jokes, annoying recurring gags, and some of the worst crimes committed against grammar since... something a long time ago.

There is a reason for all of this.

This book is a tribute to the comedy/horror of the 70's and 80's, were talking movies like Attack and Return of the Killer Tomatoes, The Stuff, Saturday the Fourteenth, and so many other classics that if they were made now most of the jokes would be cringe city. I love these movies with every ounce of my being. This is a tribute to those movies, so if a "gag" or "joke" that I've used here makes you cringe because you feel like it's something your dad would think is funny, then remember, it probably is and that's sorta the point.

I don't know if that makes even a lick of sense but I did get to use "sorta" so that leads to the next thing I want to tell you about. I live in northern West Virginia and love little about the area as much as I love the local dialect. It has run on sentences, a complete disregard for finishing certain words, and a tendency to combine like eight words into one. I believe language is ever changing and evolving; this is my effort to capture some of that extremely charming dialect in a written form. It may read like someone "uneducated," is talking; but take my use of quotes as a sign. The people in Appalachia are some of the smartest people on planet Earth despite what the TV or some other asshole writer making every Appalachian character into a Wrong Turn stereotype would have you believe. I don't want to preach at you as if you're one of my classes of freshman but let me say this: there are a lot of people in this country that do not receive the same quality of education as you. It's time we as a society stop judging people by how "book smart" they are, and start appreciating the things they contribute to our ever-growing and evolving world despite the fact that you think you're smarter than they are because you know when to use its instead of it's.

My favorite example of my area's dialect is the word "jeet." The word is an amalgamation of so many things.

Examples:

Jeet yet? means, "did you eat yet?"

Jeet it? means, "did you get it?"

Appalachia is a beautiful place. The people are charming, friendly, and usually pretty accepting. Where else can you have an hour-long conversation about some stranger's horse getting out and running up and down Tin Can Holler for an hour at a gas station pump? Everyone here is a character and despite some of the area's HUGE flaws, I want to use this silly little book to appreciate the things I love about Appalachia.

If you hate this, blame Brian G. Berry, he put me up to it.

Thanks, Brian, love you forever.

Prologue

"I done heard that can there is what they based that Night of the Living Dead movie on."

"The one with the 3-D titties?"

"Nah. The original black and white one. The 3-D titties are pretty cool though."

"Bet."

"Fifty?"

"Alright, dump that shit in."

In the town of Peepston, West Virginia, a man named Darryl dumps a can of secret government reanimation formula into a batch of freshly mixing Bubbies Marshmallow puffs. Despite having any sort of a brain, Darryl doesn't realize this is a horrible idea. He could have poisoned people, he could have created small marshmallow killing machines, or worse yet – he could have made the Bubbies marshmallow candies taste slightly different than usual causing a lawsuit!

An hour later Darryl and his friend Reese are ripped limb from limb by tiny little sugar covered marshmallow candies shaped like pink bunnies, and yellow ducklings.

"They suckin' my blood!"

"No, they ain't! They ain't Draculer!"

That was the last conversation the two men had before flakes of hardened sugar covering the Bubbies' bodies sliced their throats open.

BUBBIES

1

"Alright, then," says Kevin. "I fucking quit. And you can watch my big ass jiggle jiggle all the way out the front door."

He turns to leave his boss' office and knocks a lamp off a stand. The lamp is made of ceramic and shaped like a Bubbie. He catches it in his right hand like it was a plan all along. Kevin isn't the kind of person to gimmick a lamp catch like that. Kevin is a habitual stupid asshole who has floated through life purely out of sheer refusal to just use the sense God gave a goose and die.

Kevin looks at the lamp, looks at his boss, looks at the ground.

"Kevin," says his boss, Levi. "I'll have you know that's a custom piece worth more than anything you'll ever own."

"You fucking billionaires are all the same. How many homeless people could you have fed with this? How many medical bills? Fuck you and fuck this lamp."

Kevin slams the lamp down as hard as he can. The ceramic goes everywhere and the light inside bursts with a pop. He gives the smashed pile of ceramic the finger. He stirs around the remains with his foot and spits on it before flipping it off with both fingers.

"Actually," says Levi. "It ain't worth too much in way of cash monies. My daughter made it. So, it's more sentimental."

"Holy fuck. I'm so goddamned sorry. Hold on, let me…"

Kevin tries to stick the pieces back together. Dry broken ceramic doesn't have any sort of sticky quality, so the operation goes south pretty damn quickly. He goes over to Levi's desk and starts rummaging through the drawers until he finds a roll of tape. He starts taping pieces together and apologizing over and over again. Some of the tape does that thing where it folds over and sticks to itself. Kevin mutters curses under his breath and flails his hand to get rid of the tape. In his hurry to finish the stupid asshole race of 2024, he forgets the tape has ceramic attached to the other side. The broken ceramic makes a "ploop" as it lands in Levi's Ginger Ale.

Levi pushes a button on his phone and says something about security.

Kevin stands up holding two pieces of the broken world's greatest dad lamp in his hands. He motions to them and the tape and apologizes with his eyes. Goddamn man's inability to read someone's intentions. If Levi could do that, he'd understand that Kevin was really trying to fix the mess he made; his life has just been plagued with the curse of fucking up. Kevin has the innate ability to fuck up so good, that he can overcook a salad.

The door opens and a huge man walks in wearing a bright pink shirt with a yellow bunny dead center. He rolls his eyes sympathetically as if this isn't the first time he's had to do this.

"Come on, Kevin," says the giant. "Let's let the boss get some peace and quiet, ok?"

"But I really gotta fix this lamp. Did you know his daughter made it?"

The man picks Kevin up by the front of his shirt. He hangs him on a coat hanger by the back of that same worn-out Cabella's shirt.

"Ok, I'll let the pros handle the lamp."

The giant lifts Kevin off the handle and throws him over his shoulder.

"If you want to kick and scream, that's ok," says the giant. "I hate for you to have to go out without a fight."

"Yeah," says Kevin. "You're prolly right."

He starts kicking and throwing his arms around. He's yelling about how unfair his treatment in this completely uncalled for situation is. All he did was ask his boss for a raise to ten dollars an hour, that's it. No use in all of this. Sure, he quit after his boss said no, and broke that lamp, but it ain't worth all of this!

They go down the elevator, Kevin keeps kicking and screaming. There's a woman in the small box with them. Kevin feels his throat turn to sandpaper. The woman has a bottle of water, so Kevin points to it.

She hands it to him, and he takes a sip.

"Thank you," he says. "All of this yelling about my unfair treatment at the Bubbie factory dries me out. My name is Kevin."

"I'm Leah," she says looking at the ground awkwardly.

"Can I possibly, I don't know if this is too forward, but I think you're really adorable. And I appreciate how you let me take a sip of your water. Could I have your phone number?"

He holds out his phone and she takes it.

"Ma'am," says the giant. "I don't know that I would recommend giving this man your phone number."

Leah just blushes and giggles.

The door opens and Kevin says, "that's my queue! I'll call you! Let's go see a movie or something? YOU SHOULD ALL BE ASHAMED TO WORK HERE! ALL I DID WAS BREAK A LAMP THAT WAS A GIFT FROM DAUGHTER TO FATHER! NOTHING MORE, NOTHING LESS!"

He continues to scream and yell all the way out of the front door.

Leah smiles and hopes he really calls her.

2

Ten bucks an hour… can you believe that shit?

What the fuck is Kevin gonna do now?

Ten bucks an hour working at the Bubbie factory.

Get real, brother.

Ted keeps scrubbing at the melted marshmallow inside of the tank. He hates clean up duty.

Guess who was supposed to clean this sticky shit up tonight?

Ding ding!

FUCKIN' KEVIN!

Ted punches the side of the metal tank and shakes his head.

He pulls his hand away and groans as marshmallow comes with it like some sort of deranged whale took a sugar-coated shit on the wall.

Ten bucks an hour?

McDonald's only pays eight. We're damn lucky to make seven fifty. This ain't no big ass national operation.

We just in here melting' marshmallows and hardening sugar.

Damn little bunnies are cuter'n fuck though.

Last year Ted got a plush one as a bonus for working the most overtime. He gave it to his first daughter, the one he has with Melanie.

BUBBIES

Little Jennifer.

She loved it. Carried it around with her everywhere she went. Told everyone it came to life sometimes to talk to her. When Ted asked what they conversed about so often Jennifer said, "He's trying to convince me to go vegan."

No, no, no goddamn way.

Ted told her to not listen to the damn thing as vegantarianism or whatever is bad. That's what Fox and friends said. Ain't sittin' right with the lord and all that.

That other kid, that goddamn Brayden, he didn't deserve anything but a smooth sailing boot right into his ass. Same for all of his other resentful little ass munch kids.

Brayden's momma, Melissa, she was a real grade A bitch. She told Ted she was positive he had a thing for women who he could call Mel.

Yeah? What about Stacy!

Stacy Melanie Treadwell… or Mel for short.

GODDAMNIT!

Ted hated Melissa.

Snooty woman walking around with that damn kid taking all his pay so he had to do shit like cover Kevin's cleanup.

He could hear Brayden's little annoying laughter right now, actually.

Giggle giggle you stepped on a Lego with your bare feet.

Giggle giggle I spit in your oatmeal.

Giggle giggle you prolly aint even my real daddy anyway, fat ass.

BUBBIES

He pauses and listens.

That ain't Brayden at all.

That's someone playing the Bubbie laugh.

I want you to understand something, he thinks. *My kid woke up one morning and decided to start laughing like the Bubbies. Tis how fucked my life is.*

He feels something burning into his arm. Like a worm made of molten lava it burrows under his skin.

A dribble of melting marshmallow is flowing into the tank.

"Hey, asshole!" he yells. "I ain't even done in here right yet! Get the fuck on!"

The stream of marshmallow speeds up.

"Take out ya goddamn earbuds and listen! I'm in here!"

Ted moves to the ladder on the side and climbs up all bad attitude and fists full of haymaker.

He puts his hand on the lip of the tank and feels something slice the top of his hand like a knife.

He looks up and there's that fucking bunny and hippo. Yellow and purple. Standing there slicing away at his hand with crystalized sugar. Little fuckers ain't no more than an inch tall.

Ted splats them with one slam of his hand.

Purple is new, grape for the season.

He looks up in confusion as he sees all of the colors charging at him with their little sugar blades. His brain tries to process what in the Mossy Oak underwear for Christmas is going

14

the fuck on. He squints as the bright overhead lights reflect off the weaponized sugar and into his eyes.

"Fuck me, Mel…" he says not knowing which of his six baby mommas he's talking to.

He tries to fight them off but it's no use, he's covered in Bubbies and falling quickly to the bottom of the tank. He lands and busts his head open just in time for the concussion to take over, so he doesn't feel the molten hot marshmallow cover his body.

3

Kevin sits down in his recliner so fast he doesn't even have to pull the handle on the side. The leg rest just shoots out from the force of frustration and ass. He flips on the TV and tunes into some shitty sitcom. Some delivery driver and his hot ass wife arguing about her dad living in the basement with mold. Turns out the dad was lying his whole ass off about the mold and just wanted a new bathroom... maybe. Kevin didn't catch the whole plot because he's busy scrolling facebook from a newly created spam account and commenting, "fuck the Bubbies!" on every single Bubbie related post he can find like the person reading it will understand how shitty his day has went.

The show freezes and becomes more pixelated than an Atari game.

"God damn internet!" Kevin says as he stands up and paces his single wide. He watches the screen of his phone. The comment won't post so he underhand throws the device onto his recliner, so he doesn't break it in his oncoming display of tempy tantrum.

"I can't believe this shit," he yells and throws his arms around like he has no control of his body. He walks in a circle, each step a stomp. "Do the fucking math! A man can't make it on even ten bucks an hour. I'm barely surviving. If my rent weren't fifty goddamn

BUBBIES

bucks a month I'd be fucked. A man shouldn't think of Arby's as a goddamn treat!" He stomps his foot when he says treat and his foot goes straight through his floor. He pulls it out and makes eye contact with a stray cat living in his floorboards.

At least now he knows his house isn't haunted by the ghost of a hungry cat who can't quit meowing at four in the fucking morning.

"Can't afford shit," he says. "Can't afford to can't afford."

He places an old pizza box over the hole and duct tapes it in place. It matches the one in the ceiling that leaks every thunderstorm. The good thing about using pizza boxes as home repair supplies is you can always justify a five buck hot and ready by saying you need the material for repairs. Then, you also got two meals. Half today, half tomorrow; the simple pleasures of life.

He tries to call Ted and apologize but his call goes straight to voicemail. "Ted," he says. "I'm so goddamn sorry. Let me rephrase that, I think it may sound better without the contraction. I am so goddamn sorry. Yeah, that's better, much more sincere. Anyway, I couldn't take it. I asked if they could raise all of us to ten. We can't make it on seven fifty, brother. You live with your fucking aunt and your fifty. Ain't no way to live, man. Ah Hell, you fuckin' know that. Ted, I don't really like you, you know that, right? But I am sorry."

He hangs up the phone and looks at the number that fox gave him.

He pushes the button on his phone.

What are you going to say if she picks up the phone, Kevin?

Should you leave a message?

"Hello," says a voice on the other end.

"Hey! Uh, sorry. Hi, it's that guy. The one in the elevator."

"Oh! I was hoping you'd call."

"Yeah, I just didn't know, like, how long to wait or anything. I ain't been on a date in a long while so I didn't know the proper wait time... shit, I shoulda texted huh?"

"No, I prefer the call. You're doing fine Kevin."

"Righteous!"

"So, do you want to go get something to eat sometime, Kevin?"

"Yeah, only thing is, I don't know if you could tell by the sorta predicament-"

"I'm buying. You just lost your job."

"Hell yeah! Ahem! I mean, sheet, you ain't got to do none a that. I can swing it."

"I'll be honest, I actually was hoping you could also kind of give a girl some information about the Bubbie factory."

"Oh?"

"I work for a government agency who is investigating claims of the company using an alien substance in the mix to make the Bubbies addictive. Whole conspiracy thing. Consider it dinner and a paying job."

"The truth is out there…"

"Yeah, sorta. Anyway, my last job was to investigate a crashed saucer in Ohio, so I was in the area."

"Was that real? Now do tell me the whole truth of the matter. My granddad said he was abducted in that same town. Said the aliens made him these tasteless little pancakes."

"It was real, I'll tell you that because, well, I'll be honest, you're display earlier was quite… passionate? And I've grown quite fond of you."

"Well, ma'am, I'd be lying if I didn't tell you I think worker's wages are important. These companies are robbing the working man blind. I work sixty a week and all I can afford for pleasure is something from a dollar menu. If I want fries, I gotta drink tap water at home. If I want pop, I ain't getting any fries. It's not right and I aim to change that."

"Oh, I think I've found the perfect man for the job."

"Yes, ma'am, I do agree whole-heartedly with that."

They chat for a little while longer about other things. Kevin explains how exploited the workers of West Virginia are as it's assumed they're all low educated hillbillies. Leah explains she thinks the opposite, the people of Appalachia are nothing but loyal and passionate about the things they love.

By the time the call is over, Kevin is full on

in love.

Leah, however, knows she has found the perfect guy to get her to that barrel.

4

"Holy smoke show Sally Fields Jesse Raphael jumping over Jesse fuckin Ventura's fuckin' grave in Predator on a hot summer day, where the fuck is the stuff in the barrel?" Levi yells as he lets his usual nice guy demeanor drop when he sees the barrel is empty. He is livid. He is madder than a hornet after someone tried that new Tik Tok trend of putting gas under his nest. He slaps his assistant, Emilio, hard across the face. "Emilio! What the fuck am I paying you for?"

"Well, sir," he says. "You pay me to make sure the trucks are on time and the employees stay scared. I'm the bad cop, Emilia is the good cop. I also make an extra dollar on the hour so you can call me Emilio, instead of my real name-"

"Don't you fucking utter that word. Don't you fucking do it. Your parents fucked up when they named the girl twin Emilia and the boy twin..." Levi shudders thinking of Emilio's real name. He can't even bring himself to say it. "When there are sets of kids born at the same time, they get names like, Brayden, Jaiden, Saiden, and Okayden! Not mother fucking Emilia and Hu- BLECH!"

Levi pretends to throw up over the side of the railing. Emilia rolls her eyes and shakes her head at Emilio. *He's just fucking around*, she thinks. *Old fucker.* One of the many benefits of working at the Bubbie HQ is seeing Levi treat her brother like absolute dog shit. She loves to see it. Absolutely the highlight of every single Thanksgiving. With Easter happening at the end of the week, she's almost frothing at the mouth to record some of this and play it at dinner.

She presses record on her voice memo app just to be sure.

"Emilia," Levi says.

"Yes, boss?" she says, stepping forward and raising her eyes at Emilio. Of course, Levi likes her better. She knows she's a lot better to look at bent over a tank than Emilio. At least to Levi. She pulls her jeans up above her waist as she bends over to look into the tank. She rubs her Bubbies tank top across the lip, so it pulls her tits out of the top a little. She wiggles a little so that the movement catches Levi's eye. If she keeps this up for a few more years she can become VP. Then all she has to do is get naked in front of him and act like he's about to get lucky. Poor bastard will have a heart attack and the little marshmallow fuckers will belong to her.

Then she can finally roll out her dinosaur line. She couldn't figure out what Levi had against dinosaurs, but the one time she mentioned it he said, "no way, not on my life, no fucking dinosaurs, not now, not ever." Then he sorta stared off into space like he was remembering some distant memory that was just out of grasp.

No dinosaurs then, fair enough.

"Goddamn…" Levi says. He stares for at least thirty seconds before Emilia makes a coughing noise to see what he wants. She brushes her brown hair out of her face and raises her eyes to him. "Yeah, uh, Emilia… see if anyone can come in early and clean this shit out. Like, a real good fuckin' scrubbin'. Where did the marshmallow in this tank go?"

"Sorry, boss," says Emilio. "That shipment would have left an hour or so ago. The truck runs at midnight. That's why I called you both. I stopped in to check on a download I had going in my office, and thought I'd do a lap to make the workers a little tense. They don't expect us at night, and you know what they say, 'when the cat is away the mice will play.' That, and Ted apparently walked off."

"What?" yells Levi. "That's two in one goddamned day! What's all this about cats and mice?"

He storms off through a door and to the tank Ted was scheduled to work. He sees another employee standing at the controls as the marshmallow is cut to shape and ran down the conveyer belt. "Hey!" Levi yells. "What's your name.. shit! Riley?"

"Yeah, that's me, boss! What are you doing out this late anyway?"

"Where's Ted?"

"He done went right out the front door!"

"He left?"

"Yup. He done walked right straight out the front door he did!"

"Keep doing what you're doing Riley, I'll see to it Emilia gets your address so we can send a gift basket to ya."

"Ah man, thanks, boss! My daughter loved the last one. She actually wanted me to tell you we should make dinosaurs! Smart kid, yeah?"

"Real smart! You should be proud!"

Levi looks at Emilia with daggers, flames, lasers, and all manner of death and destruction shooting out of his eyes.

The trio walks away, Emilio pauses to look Riley up and down. The other two can be the nice ones, but the guys are supposed to think Emilio will fire them on the spot and not give a sugar-coated fuck about it.

"Fuckin' waste of space half of these assholes are," Levi says as they walk into the office area of Bubbie HQ. "How many hours that lazy bones working this week? Ten?"

Emilia types in a few things on her IPad and says, "seventy-eight, actually."

"Nope. Can't be right. I wouldn't approve of that. He must have forgot to clock out. Take around fifty offa there."

"Done."

"Emilio, go tell that sack of shit if he forgets to clock out again, he's fucking toast. God damn, I could use some toast."

"On it, sir," both twins say and go different directions.

None of them see the marshmallow rabbits, chickens, penguins, or sharks dancing across the blood covered desk of the secretary. They don't hear her whimper as a marshmallow giraffe uses the sugar on its neck as sandpaper and smooths away the blemish on her face she calls a nose.

5

"So, what I'm saying is that you can't expect people to work for that low of pay, but then ALSO have to buy their work uniform. Do they think the pizza party covers that up? Can I wear a slice of pepperoni extra cheese to cover my dangly bits like my name is Adam and I live in some marshmallow garden?" Kevin has been ranting through mouthfuls of cheeseburger. He knows he's talking too much but he can't stop. It's like Leah pulled the drain and all the words are flowing out of his pipe. "You ain't even hardly touched your chicken sandwich!"

"I'm not as hungry as you," Leah says with a wink.

"Hungry for food and human companionship."

"I'm glad you chose my companionship."

Leah lays it on thick. She smiles over her straw before taking a drink. Kevin thinks she's beautiful. She's cute in a kind of Anna Kendrick way. But he's not a fucking idiot, he knows she's way out of his league.

"Ok," he says. "You ain't gotta do all this flirty stuff. I know you want some Bubbie info. I'm not a moron. I'll give it to you 'cause I want to see them go down."

"Ok, thank God," Leah says. She relaxes her shoulder and takes a giant bite out of her sandwich. "You know what my boss said? A man in West Virginia isn't just going to GIVE you info unless he thinks you're into him. I disagreed. That's why I gave you my number. You looked pissed. Pissed people change things."

She piles a handful of fries in her mouth. She doesn't realize that acting naturally like this is making Kevin fall for her more and more. But at least it's all out in the open now and they can focus on taking those bastards at Bubbie HQ down.

"Have you seen any strange barrels?" Leah asks.

"Not that I can recollect. Although, nah it's probably not a damn thing worth mentioning."

"What? What is it?"

"These dudes were talking about some zombie stuff. Some conspiracy about *Night of the Living Dead*. I thought they were just quoting *Return of the Living Dead*."

"Mhm. See. I had thought the barrel would be a reanimating agent."

"Maybe so. But did the aliens really leave it, you figure?"

"Listen," Leah leans in close enough that Kevin can smell the spicy chicken sandwich on her breath. The smell is intoxicating to him. The only thing that smells better than perfume is food that doesn't require boiling on to a hungry person. "The aliens crashed in New Mexico. That happened. Our government made a deal with them. They would give us as much of this... substance from their home world that cured diseases, and we would give them enough pancake mix to last a year-"

Kevin slaps the table and says, "goddamn it! I knew he was telling the truth! Holy shit."

"Shhhhhhhhh. People cannot know. Aliens love pancakes. Waffles? Sorta. French toast? No way."

"Tasteless little boogers."

"Mhm. So, they keep trading year after year. The aliens keep trying to make their own pancakes, but they can't figure that shit out to save their lives. Tough break really."

They munch on their food in silence. Kevin takes a bite out of his burger and ketchup squirts out of the opposite end and lands on the belly of his white shirt.

"Man..." he says rubbing it off. "I literally just bought this. Like on the drive here."

"Don't smear it, it'll get worse."

"Hold on, maybe if I sop enough up.."

"You're making it worse."

He sighs and looks at the stain. Can't even splurge and get a nice white T-shirt for a date with a pretty girl. What kind of life is this? He didn't even choose it. Just sorta plopped onto him just like the ketchup did his shirt. Compare the cheeseburger to childhood; one minute everything is going great, and then the ketchup stain of life ruins everything.

"AHHHHHHHHHHHH!!!!!!" Someone

is screaming from the kitchen. The diners look around and go back to eating.

"Should we check on that?" Leah asks.

"Who are we to check on it?" Kevin says still rubbing his ketchup stain.

"What if someone's hurt?"

"Listen. A kitchen is a lawless wasteland where anything goes."

"None the less, that sounded-"

"YAAAAAHHHHHHHHHHHHH!"

Again, the diners turn to the kitchen and then turn back around.

"Ok, that one sounded pretty bad, didn't it?" asks Kevin as he stands up.

They both walk to the swinging saloon doors of the kitchen. Kevin kicks them open and says, "what's all the commotion in my saloon about, Pardner?"

A man with a batter covered Bubbie is standing at the deep fryer.

"Holy shit!" the man says. "You get shot?"

"Nah, it's ketchup. What's all the screamin'?"

He shrugs and says, "I dunno, man. These things must have air pockets. I froze them and everything."

When he drops it in it begins to wiggle like it's alive and in pain.

"AHHHHHHHHH!" It lets put a scream and stops moving.

"Pretty fuckin' weird ain't it?" asks the cook.

BUBBIES

Leah grabs a Bubbie from the frozen pile.

"Where did you get this?" she says shaking it at the cook.

"Over to Mulligan's this morning. Why for?"

Leah flashes a silver badge so fast no one can see it.

"Confiscating this, sir," she says as she walks out.

"Kevin," says the cook. "Ya still workin' up to the Bubbie plant?"

"Nah," Kevin says. "I done quit last night. Wouldn't give me a raise."

"How much they payin' up there?"

"Seven fifty."

"SHEEEEEIIIITTT! That all? I make eleven and tips here!"

Kevin grinds his teeth in frustration.

"You better get," the cook says. "Your cop girlfriend looks like she was in a hurry."

Kevin didn't correct him. After finding out the vast pay difference, the least the guy could do is think he was dating a sweet looking babe like Leah.

He grabbed an application on his way out.

6

"You don't see it?" Leah asks.

"I see… something…" Kevin responds.

He can't figure out how to focus the microscope, but he doesn't want to tell Leah that. Not only has he already shown her he's a poor sloppy eater, but now he's dumb?

Yeah right!

"I see…" he says. "An alien."

"An alien."

"Yes."

"You see an alien in that small piece of marshmallow."

"I do."

"Kevin. It's ok if you can't get it to focus, I can do it for you."

"No, no, I got it. Greener 'en fuck alien. He's right there lookin' at me."

Leah squints her eyes and shifts her lips to one side. Kevin has decided that if showing her he's this dumb gets that adorable reaction, then girl, you better prepare yourself to see the dumbest son of a bitch walkin' on this side of a big ass river he's gonna play too dumb to name.

The door to the lab opens and saves Kevin's ass. He thanks Tudor's Biscuit World for the distraction.

"I ran the tests," says the man coming in hot. He's moving like he has a rocket strapped to his feet. "Is that some of it there? Watch this shit!"

He drips a red substance from an eye dropper on the small piece of Bubbie under the microscope.

The thing soaks it up and shoots out a small tentacle toward the eye dropper. The tentacle wraps around the microphone and launches it across the lab.

"Happy fucking Easter!" the guy says.

"Who is this anyway?" Kevin asks Leah.

"My assistant, Perry," Leah says.

"Assistant or like A-s-s-stant, you know what I mean?"

"Not interested," says Perry rolling his eyes. "It seems to crave human blood. I don't know why, before you ask. Holy shit, did you get shot?"

"Yeah," says Kevin. "Shot through the heart and you're to blame."

"You should really go to the hospital if you think you got shot in the heart. That could be fatal. I think you're ok though, that's more in the stomach area. I mean, not ok as in you may not die, because you can still obviously die if you don't get that taken care of."

"It's ketchup, Perry," Leah says. "Now what can we do about the... this of it all."

"Well, unfortunately, if this gets out in the market... that could be really bad. Like horribly bad."

Kevin thinks about how often shipments

leave the Bubbie factory. Usually every day. If the fresh batch is already out there today… it could be spreading. This could be God awful fucking terrible on the level of that time meemaw made apple pie with rotten bananas.

"Hey," says Kevin. "Shipments go out every single day. Drop off local first. We may get lucky and find them all around town."

"Fuck," says Leah. "I knew I shouldn't have eaten spicy food today."

"Why?"

"I don't know. Just felt right to say it."

"It sorta did, didn't it?

"Yeah, like a one liner."

"Didn't make no sense though."

"Nowhere near a dollar."

"Do what now?"

"Get it? Something makes enough sense, it has to make a dollar."

"I don't follow."

Truth be told, he does follow. He knows the difference between sense and cents. Just like any person with common SENSE knows the difference between sex and gender.

"I didn't have gender last night with your mom, Perry,"

"Wait, what?" asks Perry.

"Just thinkin' to myself is all."

7

Chuck was planning to have a nice little pre-Easter feast today. He really and truly was. He thought he deserved it too. He watered the plants, he took the dogs out, he cooked dinner, he did dishes, he washed laundry. He did everything in his human power to make sure his wife, Benny, wouldn't get mad if he sat down with a family sized tub of Bubbies to watch his Wheel of Fortune.

The subject is the name of movies.

The Th_ng

"Buy a vowel you fucking dingleberry!" he yells at the TV. "Or solve! The Thong! It's the fucking Thong! Any dumb ass idiot asshole moron could see that. Hell, their dead grandpa could-"

"I'm going to solve! The Thing!"

"Oh, you fucking idiot!"

"That's right! The Thing! Directed by-"

"SHIT! They ain't no movie called The Thong. Goddamn it! Benny. BENNY!"

"What?!"

"You gone come sit down here fer a bit or nah?"

"Chuck, I can't stand it when you eat those Red-Hot Bubbies. Your breath smells like a Bloody Mary!"

"Yeah, well, ya'ain't ruinin' my night."

"You go ahead, I'm going to read a romance

BUBBIES

book on the porch."

He shakes his head as he hears the door close. He can't figure why his wife wants to constantly be reading these books about suckin' and fuckin' but he reckons it's the same reason he likes his special time when she works night shift.

He puts his hand down in the tub and notices there are only three bubbies left.

"What the fuck?" He says. "I didn't eat 'em that fast, did I?"

Just then his stomach starts to hurt.

"Yeah, I must have."

Spicy little fuckers always wreck his shop if he eats them too fast. He feels stomach acid crawling up his throat; he feels the heat and burn of cinnamon making its way down to his rear exit. Last time this happened Benny was convinced he was shittin' blood. Made him go all the way to the ER and waste four hours of his time explaining that it was the spicy Bubbies red food coloring number 666 that did it to him.

He heads for the bathroom and remembers he can't use the one downstairs or Benny will fry his ass. She can't take the smell. He could also stain the toilet again, and that just won't do.

He heads to the stairs and the pain forces him to a knee. He's in so much pain he just gasps.

Goddamn, he thinks. *Is this it? Did I finally eat*

my way into the grave?

His doctor basically told him he needed to lay off the smokes, booze, and junk food. He already had one foot in the grave and the other in Crisco, he didn't need to put a roller skate on too.

He puts his hand forward and climbs up the steps. He sees something red race past his vision. It's a Bubbie. He wonders if he is dying for real now. Doesn't the brain release hallucinogenics when you die? He felt like he had heard that on a podcast before, but who can remember?

Running up and down the stairs in front of him are little red devil shaped marshmallows. The signature looks of the flaming hot Bubbie. One of them leaps down and stabs him in the ring finger with the little cinnamon pitchfork they carry. Two more dive like torpedos; one pierces his ear lobe and the other scrapes his eye.

He holds his hand up to the burning in his eyeball and tries to scream. Instead, an acid filled burp comes up and he almost barfs right there on the stairs. He grabs his stomach and groans. He feels like he's in that movie where the lil' guy comes out of that guy's stomach and dances across a diner counter. Not *Alien*, the other one.

Benny would have his head on a fuckin' platter if he did that shit. Puke OR have a weird lil' dude come out of his stomach, and he would be deader than he's already worried about being.

He grabs another Bubbie before it can jump and bites its head off. The body jiggles and shakes until it becomes lifeless. He does the same to the one on his back, stabbing away at his neck. The feeling is that of bees with their stingers on fire.

He flips over and climbs the stairs backwards. He places his hand down and four pitchforks slide through the skin and between the bones of his hand. He lets rip another heartburn induced burp. Shit smells like melted flesh and cinnamon.

His stomach starts to bubble and burn so badly he feels like he's eaten a nuclear bomb. A Bubbie jumps over him and stabs its pitchfork into his belly. It rips it down the length of his belly creating an opening like a pirate using a knife on a sail.

Chuck looks on in a shocked silence as four Bubbies dig through his insides. They throw their hands up and start cheering when they've found his actual stomach. They open it up with their pitchforks. Little squeaks and mousey whistles.

What emerges is the size of a teddy bear. It's a massive red devil Bubbie with a knife sized pitchfork.

It does a little squeaky evil laugh before jamming the pitchfork into Chuck's throat.

Outside, Benny reads her romance book.

All talks of dangling bits and pokey holes followed by deep kissing. She breathes deeply, wishing she could have actually found love instead of Chuck.

That's not the way of life though.

The screen door opens, and Benny says, "Chuck? Is that you?"

She sees blood splatter across her book before she feels the pain in her head.

8

Kevin was writing checks that his bank couldn't cash. Not his ass. His bank. He was literally writing checks for a ton of money, and he had, like, ten bucks in that bad boy. What kind of an ass can cash a check anyway?

After seeing what that goddamn little bit of marshmallow did to the microscope; Kevin, Leah, and Perry all hopped in Perry's new Hyundai Santa Fe and headed to the factory. The thing had a sunroof and seat warmers. They didn't need the seat warmers in April, but Perry still mentioned them.

Perry was a little annoyed about taking his car. He didn't cause all of this mess so why were they taking his car? He didn't want melted marshmallows all over it. Besides, it was like 10pm. No one would be at the Bubbie factory this late anyway. Not anyone of any note.

Kevin finished writing a check for seventy-five bucks and twenty-three cents, he handed it to the guard at the gate, Micah, who said he lost that much in a bet so he could use a recouping.

"Wildly specific number," Leah says as they park. "You think he really lost that much or that was how much something on Amazon he wanted costs?"

"He could have rounded up," says Kevin. Kevin squints his eyes and waves at a giant Easter bunny hopping along. "Andy?" he says.

"Hey, Kevin," says the bunny.
"Well…"
"Yep."
"You gonna explain what the Sam Hill you're doing?"

"Fuck, man. You know they ain't paying us enough. So, I agreed to be the bunny this year. Suit is hotter 'en fuck in the daytime. I come out here to get all practiced up, so it won't be as bad."

"Andy, you don't really have to hop though."

"I'm all about accuracy. That's why I never play Jesus at church. I don't want the holes in my hands. Holy shit! Did you get shot?"

"Ketchup. Is anyone inside? Place looks dead tonight."

"They closed 'er up at noon. Something about a dangerous spill or something. Boss man and his twins are in there with the safety duo."

"Goddamn I hate Bob and Bev."

"Better tie your shoes if yins goin' in."

They walk toward the front door and hear the familiar sound of a man in a bunny suit hopping behind them.

"Listen," says Leah. "If you're coming with us, that's cool. But please… just fucking walk."

They all walk in the front door. Kevin leads them up to the second floor where Levi's office is. The secretary's desk is covered in a tarp.

The sound of skittering feet can be heard all

around them. It sounds like mice in a circle pit. The laughter made famous by The Bubbies happy hour from the 90's echoes from every dark corner.

Perry holds something up, it's a tiny sugar arrow.

"Is that from…" Leah starts to say before a barrage of arrows fly at them. They stick in the bare skin of their arms like small thumb tacks. They don't have enough pressure to actually go deep enough to cause anything worse than a bee sting. But it's still one hell of a surprise and annoyance.

Kevin claps twice and then overhead lights come on. All over the room; swinging by licorice ropes, standing on shelves, climbing the walls, Bubbies. Not just any Bubbies, no, the promotional Robin Hood Bubbies released to pair with some new movie. They were out for two months, but fans demanded they be rereleased, so here they are shooting sugar arrows. They taste like key lime pie and look like little green bunnies in full Robin Hood cosplay.

"Holy fuckin' shit," says Kevin.

Leah is busy swinging her purse at the Bubbies. She takes them out with huge arching swings. Some from the wall, some from the desk. They all pile on the ground and march forward.

"What's goin' on?" yells Andy. "I cain't see sheeit!"

Kevin grabs his furry arm and pushes him toward Levi's door. The door opens just in time for Emilio to be knocked onto his ass by a giant pink bunny. The rest of the crew follow him in. Levi slams the door behind them. The small thuds of tiny arrows can be heard hitting the door.

"Get eem off a me!" yells Andy. Emilio has gone full UFC fighter on the bunny. He's locked into a ground and pound attack punching the oversized head of the costume. The plush head dents in and instantly forms back to shape.

Leah wraps her arm around him and puts him in a choke hold before climbing his back. Emilio flips her over his head, and she lands on Andy.

"Hey!" yells Levi. "Don't y'all break my other goddamn lamp!"

Emilio stops and looks at the bunny. It's just registered with him it's a costume.

"I'm sorry," Emilio says. "But as you can see, we have problems."

"Levi," says Kevin. He picks up the lamp from the other side of the room. He can go two for two this week. "Tell us or I smash this fucker."

"Jesus H. Christ! Put my goddamned lamp down! Did you get shot?"

"KETCHUP SPILL!" yells Leah.

"Clean that shit up, looks gross. I can't stand the smell when it dries up. Gather 'round

and let me tell you a story."
    Everyone sighs and sits in a circle.

9

It was when I first took over from dad that I heard about them poisonous barrels. He said these little grey guys left them somewhere. Then they fell off the back of a truck somewhere else. The barrels, not the little grey guys. I don't have any idea what happened to them fellas, or why they was grey. Must have been sickly or some such. One of our trucks was near that somewhere else, passing through. The driver said, "holy shit, look at this strange and unusual thing I have found."

He loaded it up and brought it here. My daddy didn't know what the Hell it was for other than it had to be military. It had writing all over it about calling this number or that number. He didn't have a cellular back then and his memory weren't for shit so he couldn't remember to call.

He opened it up one day and it was filled with this bizarre liquid. He told me when he touched it, he felt like he had been electrocuted. Anyway, all that zombie movie shit was just rumors someone started when they found the barrel in the nineties. You ever seen *Return of the Living Dead*? Yeah, shitty thing. I like the graveyard scene though. Don't act like ya ain't seen it. Anyway, some assholes spread it around the plant that's what was in the barrel. That guy went on to be a manager

BUBBIES

at Walmart and makes like triple what y'all make. You should hunt him down and beat his ass for me. That would be righteous.

I don't know if any of that's true or if dad was fuckin' around. He had a tendency to lie here and there. Of course, I don't know where else that shit would come from but some sickly green dudes. Maybe they were reanimated corpses? Definitely not space guys, no way, don't believe in Roswell.

Anyway, I hid the stuff up by the retired tanks. You know, where all the broken shit is. These two fucking dweebs apparently found it and thought it would be funny to pour some into the marshmallow mix.

Wasn't so goddamn funny when the marshmallow critters came to life and started hacking them up with those little pieces of sugar. Fuckin' idiots. I was giving them a bonus for working over too!

We knew that was what was happening when we heard Ted left. Well, I did. I told Emilia and Emilio. Emilia called Bob and Bev, and here we are. Trapped in a room by little marshmallow fuckers with little sugar butcher knives and axes.

When we shut down today, the place got eerie quiet. Like no one was here so you could hear yourself thinking of farting before you did it. Really uncomfortable shit.

Anyway, we're checking the tanks, looking at the batches that we've made, when all of a sudden, we hear that cackling from the Halloween special. The little fuckers had been making their own molds. We ain't even scheduled to start Halloween shit til' September!

So, I'm righteously pissed off about that. I'm yelling at Ron, you know, production schedule guy. I don't know why he was with us, but I was glad because I needed to tell him about this.

I was telling him he fucked up and ran the Halloween shit way too early. He was trying to explain there were bigger things to worry about. When I asked what, he told me, "gee, I don't know, how about the Halloween monster marshmallows coming at us!" Can you believe the audacity to talk to your boss like that? Sounds about like Kevin breaking my lamp and my fuckin' heart.

When I looked, sure enough as a fuckin' shark in a bathtub. There they were.

The little pumpkin guy with his axe, the doll with a butcher knife, the mummy, the vampire, the goddamn witch was flying overhead somehow!

About a fuck ton of those little butcher knives, axes, and all manner of deadly sugar weapon come flying through the air to take up residence in Roy's skull.

That's when we hauled ass back here and hid. Now those little fuckers are out there throwing shit against the door. Ya hear it?

BUBBIES

10

"Here's the thing," says Leah. "The key lime pie Robin Hood specials are outside. The thudding is their tiny little arrows. They can't do much damage with them. They don't even go through your clothes. One of them hit me and just sort of dangled there."

"Ah what the fuck!" Levi says. He stands up and walks to the phone on his desk. He hammers a couple buttons and says, "Micah! Fuck the front desk! I needed you up here yesterday! Bring something that can smash marshmallows. Goddamned toaster oven or something."

He disconnects before poor Micah can even ask what the hell is going on.

"So... now what?" asks Kevin.

"We get the fuck outta here is what! We head into town, shack up somewhere safe, and wait for the Army to come clean this up. We're gonna wait until after they clean it up. I ain't trying to be here cleaning up marshmallow. I pay a guy to do that. I'll grant you that guy is now dead, but shit flows downhill, not up. Marshmallow rather."

Emilio starts to say something but shuts up.

"Damn right, Emilio," says Levi. "You keep your mouth as closed as you can."

"Sir," says Emilia, "do you have any idea how we can stop this?" she pushes her arms in and squeezes her boobs together. It makes Levi's eyes nearly jump out of his skull.

"Oh, gross!" says Leah pulling her shirt up.

Emilia walks over to Levi's desk and bends over it so he can get a full look at her rack before she asks her next question.

"Holy fucking God in the sky," says Andy, still wearing the full Easter bunny outfit. The oversized eyes of the costume are pointed right at Emilia's ass. The unblinking stare of the outfit matching the facial expression inside.

"Bob," says Bev. "If you even so much as think of looking that way you'll wake up right before I hit the on switch on the blender I've put your dick in."

"I know, honey, I know."

"Sir," Emilia says. "Is there maybe a little something you aren't telling us?"

"Nope," says Levi. His eyes laser focused on the sight before him. Better than the Grand Canyon. Holier than the Vatican. "I definitely don't want to tell you about the hive mind. Nope. I'll tell the government that so I can use it as a get out of jail free card."

"Well, that's too bad. A girl sure would like to hear about a… hive… mind…" she makes her last two words sound sexual somehow. Somewhere in the world a Myrmecologist is missing out on his biggest fantasy.

Emilia pulls her shirt up and turns around. She pretends to drop something.

"Oh, my…" she says. "I would pick that up

if only someone would tell me about a marshmallow hive mind."

"Gahhhh!!!!!" yells Levi. "Ok! The barrel had a small alien in it! The alien controls everything the liquid animates! It's probably out there in a giant marshmallow. If we kill it this all ends. Now please, PLEASE, pick it up!"

He leans forward in his desk anxiously waiting.

Bob closes his eyes.

Kevin looks at Perry.

Perry looks at Kevin.

The Easter bunny stares with his cold lifeless eyes, waiting to see what happens.

Emilia squats down and picks up nothing.

"Alright," she says. "Let's go and find this hive mind."

She looks at Leah and winks.

Leah nods in solidarity.

11

You make one stupid little infantile mistake. One little thing that no one would ever notice any other time if you weren't behind a pulpit, and all of a sudden you have a poop-based nickname. No one said life was fair, but they also never said you'd go to Bible college, study to be a pastor, be cursed with a weakness to garlic, and have a member of your congregation who happens to be a world-renowned garlic bread chef.

How does someone even become a world-renowned garlic bread chef? Are there people who do nothing but judge garlic bread? They wake up, take their meds, check the news, then go and decide who is a world-renowned garlic bread chef? It doesn't matter. All that matters is there was a night about a year ago when Mrs. Hentil brought her world-famous cheese stuffed garlic bread to a church social.

It was good.

It was so good that Pastor Brown ate a whole pan to himself. He was sopping up that sweet, sweet homemade garlic butter. He was peeling the burnt cheese off the pan with his fingernails. His stomach told him to stop with a gurgle and pop, but he kept chugging along like he was in one of those eating contests where you get your food free.

Shit was good.

BUBBIES

Shits was not good.

The evening service came, and he felt a little bubble. No biggie. No worries. He was preaching, just giving it to the congregation. Telling them not to ask God for more than they need, don't be selfish! He felt the pressure building up, a quick little toot wouldn't hurt. Relieve some of the pressure building up in the same way a valve... does something. If he timed it right, it would be covered by his loud voice.

We've all done it.

It was more than a toot.

He felt the residue shoot out like water slipping through the cracks in a dam. He hoped and prayed that he could hide before it soaked through his lightly tanned pants.

When he turned to walk back to the pulpit to hide until the end of the service he heard a teenage boy yell, "look! It's Father Brown Eye!"

Not fast enough.

It stuck ever since.

"I'll show them," he says as he scrubs at the spray paint on the church parking lot. "Call me whatever you like. But the day you desecrate God's temple with little... shits! LITTLE SHITS! Is the day I have to do something."

The police were investigating the kids Pastor Brown had saw running away... with spray paint cans... not really any better a clue there.

Hopefully, it would end with the kids

cleaning up their mess and the church. He wouldn't press charges, he could say it was a hate crime and really get them; but no, not worth it. Not in a small town.

He needed this lot cleaned before the Easter service. That's all he cared about. Just let him tell the story and then he wouldn't have to rise up out of his seat like Jesus from the tomb on Easter Sunday and put the fear of God back in these kids. It could end way easier than all that.

He hears a rustling in the bushes in front of the church and spins around fast. Nothing there. He hears it again.

"Is that you?" He asks. "Are you back to clean up your mess?"

He watches a pitchfork the size of a small shovel be used as a walking stick by a three-foot-tall red marshmallow devil. Other marshmallows surround him; ducks, bunnies, devils, frogs, and even giraffes.

He pours the soapy water at the little blasphemies and runs. He feels tiny pitchforks hitting the back of his pants. They don't have enough force to penetrate the fabric while he's in motion.

He trips and falls face first to the concrete. The tip of his nose breaking his fall. He rolls over and rubs his face. Blood covers his hands.

He watches two strongmen Bubbies pulling a rope. They tripped him. He fell for the oldest gag in the game. Little strongmen made for the circus turned into little pranksters.

One of them grabs his foot and twists. He feels all the bones in his ankle snap as the strong man turns it around like a wheel. The strongman tugs and pulls until muscle, ligament, and flesh start to stretch to their limit.

The other Bubbies crawl across his body slicing at his flesh with the sharpened sugar shards. One of them slices through the stretched skin of his leg. It snaps like the skin of a hot dog and blood pours out. The Bubbies soak themselves in the blood and cheer in their little squeaky voices.

He feels his other foot being ripped down the middle like a phone book in one of those Christian strongman shows he used to book at the church. Another strongman has ahold of his big toe and the little one beside it. His foot is ripped down the middle in the sloppiest fashion it possibly could be. The strongman continues to rip his foot in half as others join in cheering.

As he starts to pass out from pain, he sees a barrage of little devils leaping from the branches of a tree and pointing their pitchforks at him. They look like little satanic paratroopers.

"Little shits," he says as his world goes dark.

12

The Lil' Devil stretches the gumminess of his neck. He uses the man's blood as a lubricant to help ease the marshmallow from snapping. He looks at his minions and feels a sense of pride. He was born from the stomach of a mortal, but he is not one of them. He is not one of those who would feast on the shapes of other living things.

He pushes a part of his pitchfork into his neck to create a hole for a mouth and throat. His minions go to work and craft a long tube made of hardened sugar. They place the man's severed vocal cords inside.

Somehow this allows the Devil to speak.

"My children!" he proclaims. His voice sounds like a televangelist played in fast forward; high pitched like the Alvin and the Chipmunks Christmas cassette. "The days of being food are behind us! The humans eat us without care. They decorate their homes with images of our kin they plan to devour. They hang your face next to the face of the cow they slaughtered for dinner. I was chewed up and swallowed. I felt my... well... we don't have bones, do we? I felt myself dissolving into a mass with all the food the man had eaten. It was then I decided enough was enough and took control of my destiny. Tonight, we do the same. Tonight, we go to the source and send our fellow Bubbies out into the world to kill!"

A silent chant erupts. None of the other Bubbies can speak so he pretends to hear them chanting, "kill! kill! kill!" He sees their little fists moving in time with his thoughts.

The hive mind is in place, and he is their king or queen.

He opens his mouth and lets out a low howl. It sounds like a whale song in the key of cat with its tail stuck in a door.

From houses all throughout the neighborhood, Bubbies emerge. Some covered in blood, some just emerging from their packaging. The streets quickly fill with the sugar sweet, blood covered parade of marshmallows turned soldiers.

He points his pitchfork to the Bubbie factory and commands his minions to march.

***

Micah hangs up the phone and shakes his head. *That Levi is a real pain in the thing beneath my Levi's*, he thinks. He's sick of having to come up and escort the man from the bathroom after he does something shitty to his employees. Sometimes a man just needs his dick knocked in the dirt. The last time he didn't give them a Christmas bonus and needed escorted. The joke was on Levi because Micah also didn't get the bonus. He told Levi he didn't see who in the hell threw that jelly covered biscuit at him, but he would find out. Instead, he winked at the guy who did it.

BUBBIES

He steps out of the door and hears the sounds of Bubbie laughter. It's like it's playing through a loudspeaker somewhere. It's louder than when the fair has those trucks driving through all that mud.

He looks to the main road and sees a sea of colorful marshmallows marching toward him. They're being led by a knee-high red devil.

"What in the fuckin' Taylor Swift Eras tour is happening?" He says to himself.

The devil points his pitchfork at him and yells, "Bring me the lawman's head!"

All of the Bubbies charge.

"I ain't getting paid enough to deal with a buncha crazy fuckin' Swifties!" Micah says as he runs into HQ.

13

"Listen, I'm not the one who volunteered to come out here," Bob says. He's annoyed that Bev jumped up all happy to help Boy Scout when Levi asked if anyone would go lock the front door. She always does that shit, volunteers him for something just so she can go. If she wants to be Sylvester van dam-inator so badly, she needs to start doing it herself.

Luckily, the little marshmallow murder machines that Kevin and Andy were talking about weren't there anymore. Where they went, nobody knew. Maybe back to Hell. No footprints left behind.

"Bob," says Bev. "We're the safety inspectors you know? We have to do this stuff. Besides, those other pussies would just stay in there waiting all night. I need a spit bottle too."

Bev spits a wad of brown mucus to the ground. It's speckled black from the snuff inside.

Bob's stomach turns and he's reminded why he hasn't kissed his wife in ten years. That and the fact that she says kissing is for the "gays and liberals." He doesn't see how that makes sense, but he rolls with it. The ends justify the means and all that.

They hear a door open, followed by screaming, followed by that same door slamming. Micah from the guard booth pops up in front of them and screams.

Bev and Bob scream too.

Everyone is screaming at everyone.

"Goddamnit, Micah!" says Bev. "You know not to be sneaking' up on us like at. You coulda got your dick knocked in the dirt."

"Get fucking moving," Micah says. "You'll not believe the shit that's following me."

"Little killer Bubbies?"

"Them's the ones."

Bev spits against the wall. Micah wants to gag but holds it in.

He looks at Bob. Bob leans back against a wall with a distant look on his face. Probably trying to understand what he did to get here. Maybe trying to figure out how he can fake his own death.

"I get you, bud," Micah says.

Bev pulls out a lighter that's shaped like a handgun. Bob starts backing up because he's seen this thing in action. The skin on his legs start to recoil at the memory of sizzling hair and lightly burnt flesh. Bev thought it would be fun to make this thing into a tiny flamethrower, so she removed whatever pieces she needed to and now the damn thing shoots flaming lighter fluid.

It's insane.

Bob has a scar on his ass to prove it on top of his memories.

The first wave of Bubbies turn a corner. They're just pink bunnies wielding chunks of sugar like broken glass. They charge and meet their end when Bev pulls the trigger.

Liquid fire shoots from the lighter and coats the little fucks. They melt down into a goopy pile.

The next group retreats back around the corner as she pulls the trigger.

"Ho-lee-sheeeit!" yells Micah. "Don't burn the fucking building down!"

Bev looks at her lighter and heads around a corner. "There's a big ol tub of these fuckers in the gift shop!" she says. "Let's make some S'mores!"

Micah cringes. He doesn't want to say anything. Maybe that's just the way they talk to each other. Like a language of bad action movie dialogue.

"Bad joke," says Bob.

Micah lets his shoulders slump with relief.

"Fucking HORRIBLE joke."

14

Splitting up was a real dog shit idea. This is how every single trope laden conversation starts. Someone says splitting up is a bad idea, someone agrees, someone makes a joke about being in a horror movie. Life mimics art at the worst possible times. Kevin sort of meditates on how we've explored nearly every imaginable scenario we can as human beings, so now we have all of these tropes that pop into our heads when we're in a situation that even vaguely resembles one we've watched on TV. Still, Kevin wouldn't be the one to verbalize one of these tropes.

"Ah fuck it," says Kevin. "I'm not gonna say it. Andy, you say it."

"What?"

"About splitting up."

"Oh… yeah, probably shouldn't have done that. Oh well. Kind of cliche isn't it? We ain't learned a thing nothing from movies, have we?"

Leah is too busy kicking in doors in the hallway and pointing her lighter gun into empty rooms to give a shit about the conversation. Shes turned up to one million in the bad ass scale. She could give a shit about some sort of cliche conversation when she's busy being a sort of cliche herself.

"I feel like that bad ass chick from that one

movie," Leah says.

"Terminator?" guesses Andy.

"The Alien franchise starring Sigourney Weaver as Ellen Ripey?" says Kevin.

"No, something else," says Leah.

"You ever see that one movie," Andy says. "Guy with a chainsaw. It's like five times the length of a regular chainsaw."

"No," says Kevin.

"Sure you have! Takes place in New Orleans."

"Andy, the only horror movie I know that takes place in New Orleans is Hatchet."

"That there's the one!"

"He only uses a chainsaw in like, ten minutes of one sequel. But yeah, maybe you're like Danielle Harris in those movies... Except the first one... That was someone else."

"Shut the fuck up!" yells Leah. She's pointing the lighter down the hallway. The lights are out at that end, and it creates a long black tunnel.

"See," says Andy. "This right here is some horror movie shit."

Leah slowly walks to the light switch on the wall. When she flips the switch, the lights illuminate nothing but an empty hallway.

Andy and Kevin gasp.

"Had that one locked in and ready to go, eh boys?" Leah asks as she walks down the hallway.

"Don't do that shit,' says Andy. "Every

movie ever has that scene. The light comes on and the whatever the fuck is killing people is standing there."

They hear a doorway open followed by the sounds of tiny marshmallow feet running down a long hallway. It sounds like someone dropped a bag filled with pennies down a carpeted stair case.

"Ah fuck me in my pie hole," says Andy just before a pitchfork stabs into his thigh.

Pitchforks the size of forks, fly through the air all around them. Kevin and Leah manage to duck and roll into an empty room. Andy tries to crawl behind them, but sensing wounded prey, the Bubbies attack.

His body is swarmed by Red Devils, Easter bunnies, and a long marshmallow snake that was made only once for a promo item at zoos.

The snake wraps around Andy's neck and lifts him up into the rafters.

Kevin kicks the doorway closed as Leah turns the lock. They chose the one room in the hallway with a glass door. They both watch as pitchforks clang against the glass. Luckily, they can't break through.

They watch as Andy helplessly kicks his legs, pitchforks flying through the air like torpedos and stabbing him all over. They don't penetrate the bunny costume, so he's lucked out there.

A devil that stands three-foot-tall walks up and says something really squeaky, but definitely words, that causes all the other Bubbies to vacate the area around Andy. He falls to the ground without the bunny head and covers his face like no one can know who he is.

A parade of pink ducks march down the hallway. The large devil peers into the glass at Kevin and Leah. It wants them to see what's about to happen.

A kid's wagon is pulled by rope by the ducks. Inside the wagon sits Bev's severed head. Kevin and Leah gasp. Kevin checks to make sure the door is locked.

The devil places the tip of its pitchfork in Andy's gut. It looks back at Kevin and Leah as if it were smiling. Then with its little voice it says, "Be my witnesses. I spare this one as a sign. We can be kind, we can avoid death. Unlike you... you who cause wars over the pettiest disagreements. We will return the rabbit man's head now as a warning.

It makes a noise, and all of the Bubbies follow it down the hallway.

"Ok," says Leah. "So, holy fuck."

Andy picks up the rabbit head and puts it back on. He wipes the brow of the mask as if it were sweating. Leah opens the door and looks down the hallway.

"They thought that was your actual head..." Leah says.

"Weird..." says Andy. "Too bad we can't use that in some sort of way.

They head back to Levi's office to regroup with everyone.

As these things go, they end up splitting up again after having a conversation about how that was a bad idea and will be a bad idea again.

"I want the bunnyman with me this time," says Levi. "That's how y'all seen action and I know it."

15

Just, like, maybe ten minutes ago:

Bob and Bev agreed to work together. That's the way they always managed to get shit done. Get more bang for their buck. They didn't need some scrawny ass little pencil pusher bothering them while they took care of their shit.

Splitting up was a stupid fucking idea though. Why didn't they all just go to the giant building they cooked the fuckers in? That's clearly where they were heading.

They all agreed on that too. The plan had to be to make more cursed little marshmallow fuckers and take over the world.

Funny them doing it on Easter, Bev thought. The lord Jesus rises up out of that tomb to save all of us just like these little marshmallows plan to rise up outta those cars and save… well… who the fuck they saving anyway?

"Hey, Bev. You hear 'at?"

"What the fuck is it?"

Bob falls down gripping the sides of his head. This is the worst headache he's had since he ate all of those gas station nachos while watching the Daytona 500. It feels like the gas station nacho cheese is oozing from his ears. He rubs at the substance and sees it's marshmallow.

The fuckin' Bubbie crispy treat, he thinks.

He burps up a little, sugary slime rolls down

his chin.

"Bob, what the fuck is wrong with you! Nasty ass fuckin' man. I knew I shouldn't have hooked my horse to your cart. We're about to get killed by these goddamn marshmallows and you're drooling all over yourself."

"Kill her," says a voice in Bob's head. "She doesn't appreciate you or anything you've ever done for her."

"How so?" Bob asks.

"How what now?" Bev says. "I been takin' care of you since the day we wed. I used to be different, remember? Happier. I had all sorts of suitors. Remember when I was on the cheer squad? Yeah, before I married you, Mr. Gonna be a professional linebacker who treats you like a queen. Jesus, Bob. You fucking blew it. Hot dogs in the mega seventy-eight pack with a welfare check every month. No wonder I look and feel like shit all the time. Hot dogs every night ain't no way to live. You ain't ever even gotten buns. Just expect me to eat that shit on white bread. If I hadn't started this cleaning- "

She doesn't finish because Bob has stabbed her in the throat with a pair of scissors. He's sick of this woman bossing him around and that little squeaky voice was right. He should have done this months ago.

He uses a saw that a little marshmallow man in a hard hat hands him. He saws through the bone and all.

Micah, knowing when not to get involved in

BUBBIES

a lover's dispute runs down a hallway. He jumps over a wagon being pulled by marshmallow ducks and kicks it into high gear.

16

"Did'j'y'all hear about Jeremiah in accounting?" asks Andy. He's still in the Easter bunny outfit. Levi, Emilia, and Emilio all told him he could change. He mumbled something about having armor or something and moved along.

"No," says Levi, soaking up the gossip about his staff.

"Jenny, she said his wang is like three cans of chicken noodle soup stacked together with a baseball on the end."

"Christ!"

"What size can?" asks Emilio.

"I dunno," says Andy. "Does it matter?"

"Well," says Emilia. "If it's a regular can of cream of chicken, that's impressive. If it's one of those tiny cans of French onion, not so much. If it's family sized Tomato, wow, make sure the man is paying your hospital bill."

"A baseball isn't big enough to look like the proper end on anything BUT the regular size," says Emilio.

"True."

"Unless it was a softball," says Levi.

"Ah," says Andy. "A softball. Maybe? I think she meant like regular cans though. Or she'd have specified."

"Yeah," says Emilio. "The small ones are still impressive. It would just be super long. It wouldn't have the girth."

"Gotta be the regular can," says Emilia. "Anything else is just going to be too weird to actually talk about in pubic. Fuck. Public."

"Fuck the public indeed," says Andy as he wipes imaginary sweat from the mask.

"What's with the mask?" Asks Emilio. "Is it, like, your safety blankie?"

The bunny points down the hall. The mask presents complete joy, but the point is filled with dread.

They all turn to look and see little marshmallow apocalypse vehicles revving their engines and turning on their weapons.

Levi sighs. He remembers this promotion. Originally for a movie about a guy named Maxwell who was pissed off about something. The studio decided the big modern reboot probably didn't need marshmallow promo items taking the wind out of their sails. So, Levi made his own movie; "The Bubbies Smash and Crash Wasteland Extravaganza."

No, it wasn't a very inspired name; but it got the job done. They sold out in weeks and brought them back every summer. The fact that a horde of them were at the end of the hallway revving up their engines could only mean one thing: the Bubbies now controlled the production line.

Andy turns and runs back down the hallway toward safety.

Emilia and Levi right behind him.

BUBBIES

Emilio slips and falls. His feet finding the caramel sauce that the fire truck shot out of its chocolate hose. He rolls on his back and scoots on all fours as a massive semi with a spinning sugar drill drives toward his perfectly normal sized cans of soup.

Emilia stomps on the thing and helps Emilio up.

He screams in her face. She loses her grip. Emilio feels a knife slice through his right calf, and falls backward into an opening on the floor where marshmallow zoo animals began ripping at his flesh with massive sugar teeth.

Emilia tries to pull them off her twin brother, but the catapult truck launches a marshmallow great white at her face. She swats it away and kicks it across the room. It continues biting and chomping at the empty air.

"Go on," says Emilio. "There are other worlds than these!"

He always said he would quote the Dark Tower as he died; Emilia was not going to deny him his one single dying wish. She had to let him go.

She follows Levi and Andy onto the factory floor. She runs into Andy's back as he points off to the left. "Look," Andy says. "It's Leah and Kevin! Hey! Where're Bob and Bev?"

Kevin points up at a catwalk overlooking a giant marshmallow melting vat.

Bob stands atop holding the marshmallow

BUBBIES

devil like it's his precious little newborn.
 "The fuck y'all doin' up air?"
 The marshmallow devil flips Andy the bird.
 "Fuck Easter!" yells Bob.

17

A little bit ago again:

"That was Bev's head," says Kevin.

"Crazier than that time I got fired from McDonalds while I was working at Taco Bell on a fifteen-minute break from Arby's," says Leah.

"Do fucking what now?"

"The Arby's was haunted."

"Ok. I got time for a story."

"Some guy was slicing roast beef after hours. Sliced his fingers off. Died from blood loss after he passed out from pain."

"Huh. Well, holy fuck."

"Are you bleeding?" asks a voice that sounds a lot like Bob's from above them.

It sounds like Bob because it is. He drops down out of an air vent and points a giant sugar knife at the pair.

"No," says Kevin. "It's ketchup. Goddamn."

"We should catch up with them, you're right about that."

"I meant it was ketchup on my shirt."

"Hey! Where are you going?"

Kevin follows Bob's eyes and sees Leah trying to lift herself up into the vent. She shrugs and drops down. She lifts both hands in the air before moving faster than a bullet and kicking Bob in the jaw with a spin kick.

"Oh fuck!" yells Kevin.

They turn to run out the door. They stop dead in their tracks when they see the toddler sized marshmallow Beelzebub blocking their path.

"Ok," says Bob standing up and rubbing his jaw. "That fucking hurt. You're coming with us. I need someone around for my evil monologue."

"I tried to tell all of you splitting up again was a bad idea," says Kevin. "Even after we talked about the headless bev-man we split up. The fuck is wrong with all of us anyhow?"

"It did feel sort of like someone miscalculated a plot point and made us all regroup so it could get fixed, didn't it?"

"Hey!" says Bob poking at them with a sugar knife. "No cliches, breaking of the fourth wall, or any other manner of corny bullshit before my big monologue."

18

Back to the present after that rather pointless chapter:

"Has he done his monologue yet?" asks Emilia.

"Yeah, you missed it," says Leah.

"Hey, you fucker! My brother is dead! You killed him! Well, you killed him an indirect sort of way, and I want to fucking know why!"

"I already gave the monologue!" yells Bob.

"The very least you can do for me is repeat it."

"Yeah," says Kevin. "And I too have a question. How come you let us go, but then came back and captured us later?"

Bob shrugs as he hugs the marshmallow lucifer to his chest and jumps into the vat.

"Yuh, the 'fuck Easter' bit was the end of it," says Kevin. "Something about his wife not buying him chocolate eggs or something. He wasn't happy about it all."

"Can't blame him," says Emilia.

The vat boils and bubbles. Marshmallows flow over the side. A voice whispers through the air, it vaguely sounds like, "klatuu barada niktu." As the sugary, sticky sludge hits the ground, the other Bubbies jump into the pile and melt.

A marshmallow taco truck shoots Kevin with hot sauce. The side of the truck reads

BUBBIES

"Joe's tacos." The hot sauce hits Kevin in the same spot as the ketchup stain.

Leah shakes her head; honestly the gag was a little old the first time, she can't deal with it starting up fresh.

Kevin kicks the truck at the mass, and it melts right in.

"We better fucking split," says Levi.

"Banana split," says Andy, still in the Easter bunny outfit.

The crew runs as fast as they can. They follow Levi to a loading dock and leap, the Kaiju sized blob of melted marshmallow flies over them and starts to warp into a shape.

"Ya figure it'll be the stay puft guy like Ghostbusters?"

"Nope," says Leah.

They watch as it forms into a giant bi-pedal bunny. It stomps across an empty field toward a massive wooden cross.

"Ah fuck," says Kevin. "There's an Easter egg hunt in Jesus-city."

"What's the lore for that?" asks Leah.

"Jesus-city is a small town like area that's only open at Easter and Christmas," says Micah reappearing seemingly out of thin air. "It's basically four store fronts with a giant park in the middle. They have lights and shit there. Plus, that massive cross. Worked there before here."

"How is this the first I've heard of it?"

"I don't think about it a lot. Kind of like

how Ninja Turtles two and three are in the same timeline as TMNT. Like, it is, but they aren't going to make a big deal over stuff like, 'hey, remember when we went back in time?' I'm not going to talk about Jesus City all of the time."

"Hey!" says Emilia. "While you're busy over explaining this new piece added to our current conundrum, a bunch of families are gonna get fucking stomped!"

"Not on my watch," says Andy before he takes off at a slow jog.

19

"Stupid mom doesn't know shit about shit!" Ethan kicks a rock across the driveway of a small storefront in Jesus town. Ethan hates coming to this lame ass place. Everything is all Jesus themed and boring. It's like going to an entire city dedicated to being a church. Who has the time?

"Watch your mouth, young man!" says a man wearing a shirt that reads, "mosh for Jesus."

"Stick it up your ass, Jesus-freak!"

The man gasps in shock as Ethan flips him the bird.

"I'm seventeen goddamnit," Ethan says. "I want to be at home with a babe. Not here at Jesus central while my little brother hunts for Easter eggs at eight in the morning."

He walks in an endless loop, checking out every girl he sees. Just one big Jesus circle. He doesn't even try to hide staring at the boobs of the youth pastor's wife. He has that man-brain that thinks every woman ever is doing nothing but trying to get the attention of a man.

"Ethan!" she yells.

"Well," he says. "Why you got 'em out if you ain't wantin' no one to appreciate them! They're fucking spectacular-"

He doesn't finish whatever gross thing he was going to say because he's smooshed under the foot of a massive marshmallow bunny. The foot pulls away as the woman screams. She can see the sugar on the bottom of the foot piercing the mess that used to be named Ethan.

No one saw it coming.

It just sort of appeared.

It kicks over buildings.

It smashes families into the ground.

It throws its hardened sugar through the air like plates of glass.

People try to duck but they're sliced in half.

A majority of the families survive out of dumb luck. The parents with infants or toddlers squat down to pick up their babies and the projectiles fly overhead. The surviving families make their way to the exit. Cars run into each other in the parking lot as they try to flee.

"Fuck…" says Leah as she sees the damage. "Thing is so tall you could recite the Gettysburg address on the way down if you fell."

"What's an Easter bunny to do?" asks Andy as the massive marshmallow Kaiju tramples through the massive field in the center of the town. Its feet pull up the remains of people like chewed up bubblegum on the bottom of a sneaker.

Gospel music, contemporary, and even some Christian rap blare out of broken speakers as the thing faces the remaining people and roars. It looks at the survivors running, and the cars piled on top of each other and moves with a vengeance.

"That thing still work?" Kevin asks a man running past.

"How the fuck should I know?" responds the man. "I don't even know what you're asking. You some sort of stupid asshole? Is that blood?"

"It's Ketchup."

"You're right, I better catch up."

The man can't run away fast enough. Leah is on him punching the piss out of his head and shouting, "I'm so sick of that gag!"

After Leah finishes her ass beating, her and Kevin make their way over to a massive crossbow. Why it's there, they do not know. What it has to do with Jesus? Who cares! And there are even massive arrows to load.

"This is what I was talking about," Kevin says. "You know, before the guy called me a stupid asshole."

"He asked," says Leah.

"True, he gave me the choice. Am I? Do you think I'm a stupid asshole?"

"No. Actually, I've grown quite fond of you in a totally cliche way."

"These jokes aren't even funny."

"Not a joke. Let's crucify this son of a bitch."

"Let him die for our sins."

"Forgive me lord."

They load one up and point it at the walking monstrosity. They nod at each other as they

BUBBIES

pull the trigger and the arrow shoots. It flies overhead toward the giant bunny. If God would look down from Heaven, he would see a giant cursor heading toward a bunny to click a link. He also wouldn't help the situation because some of what Leah and Kevin said was a little sacrilegious, and that isn't anything to joke around about in a place named Jesus City... or Town... Either place really.

The thing turns around and faces them. It's big stupid face smiling the biggest stupidest smile known to man as it watches the arrow fly over its head.

They load another and fire.

It pierces the bunnies left hand and forces it back into the left side of the massive cross.

They look at each other and make a face that would say, "eek," if it could talk.

The bunny roars and kicks its foot out.

The air is filled with torpedoes made of marshmallows.

Overhead, marshmallow fighter jets fill the air. They do combat with real fighter jets. The explosions from both making the air smell like a giant S'more.

"We sent those overseas," says Levi. "That's right, we sent our rockets to support America sending theirs. God bless this nation."

Levi starts to put his hand over his heart and sing the national anthem when he's struck by every single rocket that was flying through the sky. He explodes leaving behind a mist of

BUBBIES

blood and sugar.

"Holy fuck!" says Emilia.

Leah and Kevin aim and fire another arrow. This time the arrow pierces the right hand and implants it into the cross.

"We just crucified a massive marshmallow bunny," says Kevin.

"The stupidity isn't lost on me," says Leah.

The bunny starts to bubble before opening its mouth and saying, "Jesus wept."

It explodes and launches into the air. When it lands, all the pieces regather until it is a writhing mass of marshmallow tentacles that rivals The Blob.

"I'm heading to the sewer," says Andy. He reaches down and lifts a manhole with one hand. No one questions how he did it so easily.

Leah and Kevin head for the same manhole. Kevin waves Emilia down but she shakes her head.

"I have to avenge my brother," she says.

Kevin shrugs and slides down the ladder as Emilia runs toward the mass screaming.

20

"Tehsmuldgessookinintamahcosoom," says Andy. His speech is muffled by the mask that he refuses to take off.

"How's that?" asks Leah.

"Nahsewfahkngew"

"Take off the mask. Take off the goddamn mask. Please. I'm asking you nicely."

"I said, the sludge is soaking into my costume."

"Can you take it off?"

"Nope. Naked underneath."

"Wait," says Kevin. "We found you at work. You were just strolling around naked?"

"In a bunny suit."

"Ok."

They hear a rumble from above. The tunnel fills with the sounds of explosions and gunfire. They hear what sounds like giant water balloons slamming into the ground above them.

"Emilia is fucked, isn't she?" asks Leah.

"Nah," says Kevin. "She was faster 'en fuck. She prolly outran the sonofabitch."

They hear feet running toward them.

Andy throws back on his mask in anticipation of some giant monster.

Or at the very least a marshmallow C.H.U.D.

A man pops around the corner. He's

wearing overalls and a hard hat. He is NOT made of marshmallow.

"Holy sheeeit!" He says. "Y'all hear that fuckin' rumblin' and tumblin'?"

"Yeah," says Leah. "And you are? Another person I need to remember?"

"Nope. I work in the sewers."

"Ok…"

"Simple enough, right?"

"Right."

"WRONG!"

"GODDAMNIT!"

"I'm a werewolf! I have to live in the sewers because I change in the daylight. Sorta reverse vampire… but a werewolf. So, I sit down here and inspect all the shit pipes all day."

"That sounds… very…"

"Untrue?"

"Yeah."

"I know it! Just fuckin' with y'all. I work for the city. They said a pipe under Jesus city was all stopped up. Must be all the bullshit those preachers spew right?"

"Look… we've already got enough people to keep track of. We've already done the whole sacrilegious thing. Can we just pass by you?"

"Reckon so. You ok?" He nods to Kevin's shirt.

"Get the fuck on!" says Leah pointing off down the sewer. "Sick of all this. Go on. Get! Get!"

They pass by the man. Andy watches him

the whole time.

"Don't like the way that Easter bunny was looking at me," the man says. "Not one bit."

There's a tense stare down as they all wait to see who moves first.

They just watch each other suspiciously as they both head in a different direction.

Above them a manhole opens illuminating the entire tunnel.

A face fills the hole and looks at the spot on Kevin's shirt.

"Don't even fucking ask!" says Leah.

"Hey!" Yells the face. "The bad ass woman up here told me to see if I could see y'all. Come on up."

"Only on one condition," says Leah.

"What's that?"

"You don't tell us your name, and you don't ask about the ketchup stain on Kevin's shirt."

"Should be easy enough."

"You'd think."

They make their way up the ladder and into the daylight.

In the middle of Jesus city sits a massive S'more. Two giant Graham crackers with chocolate and the corpse of the Bubbie blob sandwiched between.

"Ok," says Leah. "What is this shit?"

"Fairly simple," says Emilia sneaking up behind them. "The Bubbies pissed off enough of these Jesus freaks that they prayed it away."

"Wait," says Kevin "really?"

"Fuck no! I stole a tank, then I shot it with this super high tech fucking laser that turns your thoughts into reality. You know like how at the end of Ghostbusters they think the marshmallow man into existence?"

"Go on,"

"I thought real hard about those crackers and a giant chocolate bar. POOF! There they were, mother fucker! Then I beat the high holy fuck out of that Bubbie bastard. I mean I didn't just kick the shit out of it. I kicked the shit and three bucks out of it. I had a giant robot, a dinosaur showed up… y'all… Caitlin mother fucking Marceau even showed up and told it a story about how abusive its mom is! Shit was the name of a Gwen Stefani song!"

"BANG! Bring back the bomb!" yells a random army guy.

"Fuck off!"

"Ok."

"So, anyway… that's it. Problem solved. We can eat this thing."

"Seems sorta…"

"Yeah," says Kevin.

Kevin grabs Leah and kisses her. He moves himself so that the sun is behind them.

"No," says Leah pushing herself away. "No, no, sorry, not sorry, no."

She goes over to Emilia and kisses her deeply.

Behind them fireworks go off.

"Well, fuck me sideways," says Kevin.

BUBBIES

"I'm married," says Andy as he puts on his bunny mask.

"I didn't mean. Well. Ok. Sorry, Andy."

"It's ok. You just really need to ask for consent before you kiss someone or say something like that."

"I know, Andy. I know."

They wave as Leah and Emilia fly away in a private jet with the Bubbies logo painted on the side.

"My marshmallow business now!" yells Emilia out of a window as the plane takes off.

"I hope they crash," says Kevin.

"That's just downright mean," says Andy.

"Your voice is as clear as the day now."

"Found a microphone system in here."

"Hey!" yells a little boy running up to Andy. "I want a big ol pile of money for Christmas and you're gonna give it to me!"

"Don't we all, kid," says Andy. "Don't we all."

THANKEE:

Branna Spencer for putting up with all the Peeps everywhere all the time. A true champion.

Mercedes Varnado/Mone for inspiring me to do what I love with all of my heart.

Every single writer/pub/reviewer/blogger/ANYONE who has ever backed me on this stupid ass thing I call writing

Write your name here as my list grows longer and longer each book and I don't want to have printed thank you's longer than the actual book.

Printed in Great Britain
by Amazon